Topic: Useful Tools   **Subtopic:** Tools

Notes to Parents and Teachers:

Children enter school with a vast understanding of spoken language, but written letters and words are not as familiar. The best way to get children reading is to teach them how to decode words. Begin by teaching that words are made up of phonemes (sounds). Then, teach children the letters that stand for those phonemes. As their decoding abilities get stronger, they will begin to comprehend what they are reading as well. These skills will help them become proficient readers.

Bookends for the Reader!

Here are some reminders before reading the text:

- Look through the pages of the book to get a sense of the story and make a connection to something you already know.

- Focus on letter sounds instead of letter names. Practice sounding out each word letter by letter (sound by sound) and blending the sounds to read words.

- Some words may need to be memorized because they are not decodable.

Words to Know Before You Read

airplane
box
car
door
house
idea
wheels
wings

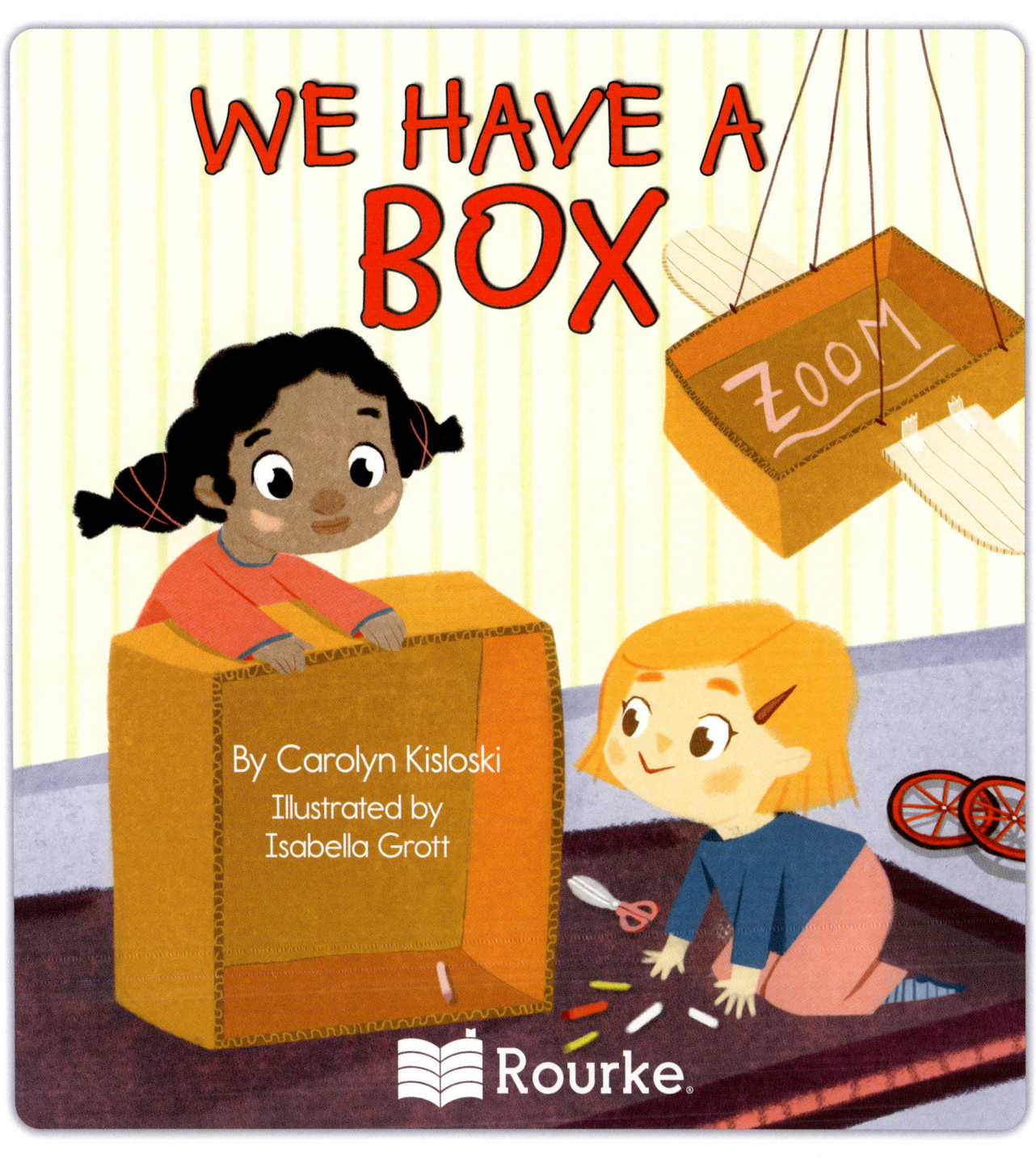

We have a box.

What can we do?

I have an idea!

Let's put on wheels.

Wow, look at that!

It is a car.

We have a box.

What can we do?

I have an idea!

Let's put on a door.

Wow, look at that!

It is a house.

We have a box.

What can we do?

I have an idea!

Wow, look at that!

It is an airplane.

Bookends for the Reader

I know...

1. What do the children have?

2. What do the girls put on the box first?

3. What does the box look like with the wheels on it?

I think ...

1. Have you ever made your own toy?

2. What did you need to make your toy?

3. What would you make if you had a box?

Bookends for the Reader

What happened in this book?
Look at each picture and talk about what happened in the story.

About the Author

Carolyn Kisloski has been a life-long teacher, currently teaching kindergarten at Apalachin Elementary School, in Apalachin, NY. She is married and has three grown children. She enjoys spending time at the beach and the lake, playing games, and being with her family. Carolyn currently lives in Endicott, NY.

About the Illustrator

Isabella was born in 1985 in Rovereto, a small town in northern Italy. As a child she loved to draw, as well as play outside with Perla, her beautiful German Shepherd. She studied at Nemo Academy of Digital Arts in the city of Florence, where she currently lives with her cat, Miss Marple. Isabella also has other strong passions: traveling, watching movies and reading - a lot!

Library of Congress PCN Data

We Have a Box / Carolyn Kisloski

ISBN 978-1-68342-708-7 (hard cover)
ISBN 978-1-68342-760-5 (soft cover)
ISBN 978-1-68342-812-1 (e-Book)
Library of Congress Control Number: 2017935354

Rourke Educational Media
Printed in Ningbo, Zhejiang, China
06-0202512936

© 2018 Rourke Educational Media

All rights reserved. No part of this book may be reproduced or utilized in any form or by any means, electronic or mechanical including photocopying, recording, or by any information storage and retrieval system without permission in writing from the publisher.

www.rourkebooks.com

Edited by: Debra Ankiel
Art direction and layout by: Rhea Magaro-Wallace
Cover and interior Illustrations by: Isabella Grott